ROAR!

A great big thank you to . . .
Alison, Christine, Emma, Mary, Meryl,
Stephanie and Strawberrie for all the support
and trust bringing this book to life!

BLOOMSBURY CHILDREN'S BOOKS
Bloomsbury Publishing Plc
50 Bedford Square, London, WC1B 3DP, UK

BLOOMSBURY, BLOOMSBURY CHILDREN'S BOOKS and the Diana logo are trademarks
of Bloomsbury Publishing Plc
First published in Great Britain 2020 by Bloomsbury Publishing Plc

Text and illustration copyright © Katerina Kerouli 2020

Katerina Kerouli has asserted her rights
under the Copyright, Designs and Patents Act, 1988, to be identified
as the Author and Illustrator of this work

A catalogue record for this book is available from the British Library

ISBN 978 1 4088 9129 2 (HB)

1 3 5 7 9 10 8 6 4 2

Printed and bound in China

All papers used by Bloomsbury Publishing Plc are natural, recyclable products from wood
grown in well managed forests. The manufacturing processes conform to the environ-
mental regulations of the country of origin.

To find out more about our authors and books
visit www.bloomsbury.com and sign up for our newsletters

ROAR!

Katerina Kerouli

BLOOMSBURY
CHILDREN'S BOOKS

LONDON OXFORD NEW YORK NEW DELHI SYDNEY

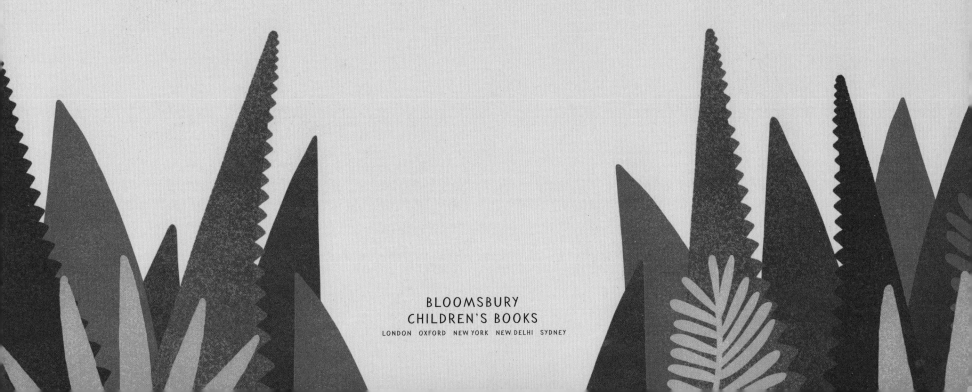

Tiger, Tiger,
is that you,
hiding in
the tall bamboo?

Such stripy stripes,
such sharp,
sharp claws,
such furry ears,
such big
wide jaws!

Crocodile, Crocodile,
do you lurk there,
with your beady
black-eyed stare?

Such pointy teeth,
your tail so long,
such scaly scales,
and jaws
so strong.

Snake, Snake,
is that you I spy,
slithering and
sliding by?

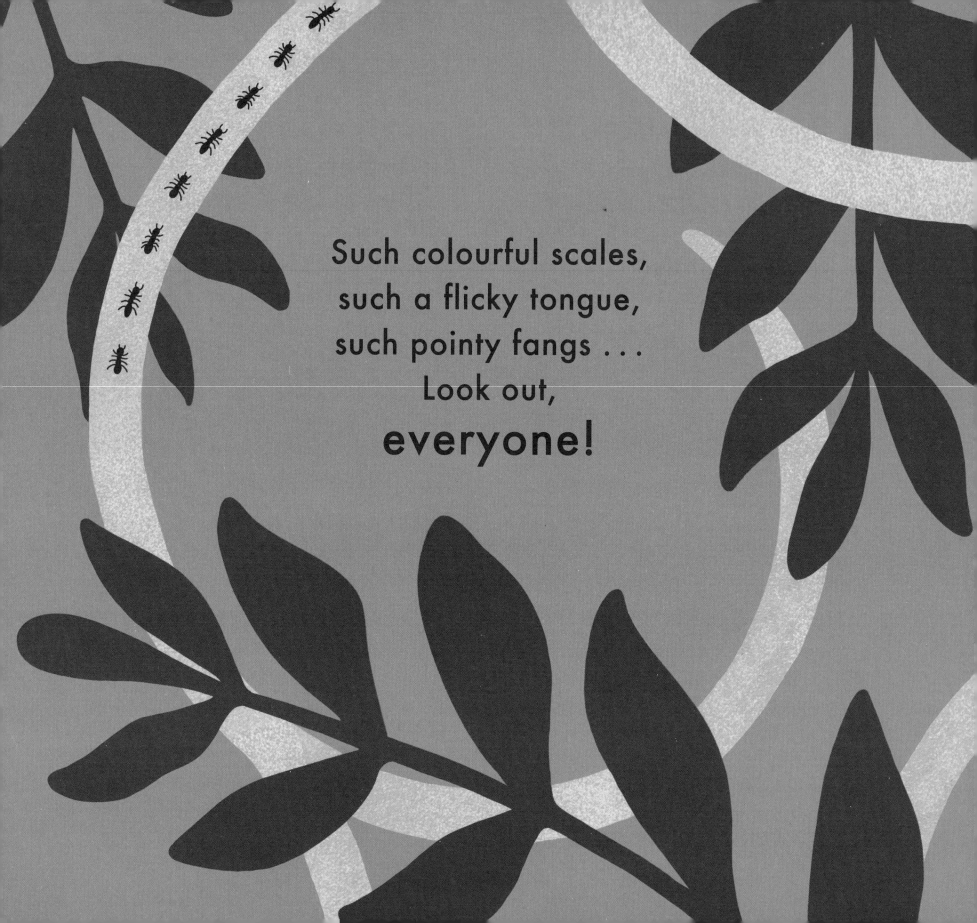

Such colourful scales,
such a flicky tongue,
such pointy fangs ...
Look out,
everyone!

Monkey, Monkey,
in the tree,
is that your
curly tail I see?

Such soft brown fur,
such a hairy chin,
such sparkling eyes,
such a
cheeky grin.

Lion, Lion,
with your golden mane,
are you on the
prowl again?

King of the jungle,
so strong and proud,
your gaze
so fierce,
your call
so loud.

The end!